Race Further with Reading

The
CALAMITOUS
COOK

By Rachel Delahaye

Illustrated by Janet Cheeseman

W

CHAPTER ONE
A Funny Phone Call

Donald was sitting by the fire with his cat curled in his lap, watching a programme about dogs. It was the perfect way to relax after a terrible day.

Donald was a children's party entertainer –
and not a very good one. This last party
had been the worst ever. He had tried hard
to entertain, but the children booed his
terrible jokes and stole his juggling balls.

Then they threw food at him – cupcakes, crisps, sausage rolls ... and eggs. Donald could handle most foods in a food fight, but not eggs. Being hit with an egg was horrible.

"Timmy," Donald said to his cat. "I don't want to be Tartan Blanket, Children's Entertainer, anymore. That egg did me in. I've had enough."

Just then, the phone rang.

"Is that Martin Banquet?" the voice on the telephone said.

"Er, yes?" said Donald, who thought the caller had said his name wrongly.

"I'd like to book you for a party."

"I don't do parties anymore," said Donald, nodding to Timmy.

"But this is a very special party to celebrate
the fiftieth birthday of The White Apron,
the finest restaurant in the country.
The founder, Antonio Maccaronio,
will be there."

"It's not a children's party, then?" Donald asked.

"No," said the voice. "And you will be paid very well." The caller then gave Donald a sum that made his eyes pop open. With that amount of money, he would never need to work again. He could spend all his days with Timmy.

"I'll do it!" Donald declared.

"Excellent. Thank you, Mr Banquet."

"It's Blanket," Donald insisted, but the caller had put the phone down.

CHAPTER TWO
The White Apron

The day of the party arrived. The White
Apron staff were in a spin. Gustav, the
snooty manager, was giving orders.

"Lay the tables!" he said. "Don't forget the olive oil. Remember the salt and pepper," he snapped. "And flowers – we need flowers on every table!"

Gustav turned to Ellie, the kitchen assistant.

"Do we have everything our world-famous chef might need to make a celebration dinner?"

"Yes, Sir," gulped Ellie, eager to please.

"We have everything, from fish to fennel, beetroot to butter."

Ellie was about to list more ingredients but the front door flew open. The chef had arrived! Gustav fixed his bow tie and put on his biggest smile.

"Welcome to The White Apron," he said with a low, sweeping bow.

The staff gawped. The man in the doorway looked very strange.

"Why is he wearing a tartan hat?" said one.

"Why is he wearing a tartan blanket?" said another. All of them wondered why he was wearing shorts with long tartan socks, but Gustav hushed them with a stern look.

"Our celebrity chef is eccentric, and he has a fearsome temper. Don't say anything, just do as he says!" he whispered.

"This way to the kitchen, Sir," Ellie said nervously, taking Donald's arm.

"What will I be doing in there?" asked Donald.

"Just do what you do best," she said. "I'll be your assistant."

STAFF ONLY

CHAPTER THREE
The Tablecloth Trick

The party guests poured in. Donald gulped

when he saw their expensive suits, dresses,

gold watches and diamonds. At least

they're not children, he thought and

stepped forward with confidence.

"Ladies and Gentlemen, I am Tartan
Blanket. Are we all ready to have a good
time?" There was a stunned silence.

Gustav quietly explained to the guests that
the chef was famous for his odd behaviour –
the stranger his mood, the better the food.

Back in the kitchen, Donald didn't know quite what he was supposed to do. The balloons would pop on the ovens, and where would he find room to juggle? He called for Gustav.

"Shall I start with a few jokes?" he asked. Gustav peered down his nose and blinked with confusion.

"Sir, I would suggest starting with some canapés."

"You want me to serve them tents?" Donald wrinkled his nose.

"Not canopies. Can-a-pays!" Gustav explained, eyes bulging in disbelief.

"It's French ... for nibbles!"

Donald nodded and turned to Ellie.

"For some reason he wants me to cook! What would you suggest?"

"I would suggest little toasts with olives and tomatoes, Sir." Ellie tried not to giggle.

"Excellent idea," Donald clapped, and he told Gustav, who looked relieved. But not for long. Gustav froze in horror as he watched Donald assemble the plates of nibbles on the end of poles ... and spin them!

"Catch them in your gob," Donald called.

"Hands behind your back, no cheating!"

The guests stepped forward awkwardly with their mouths open. They tried to catch the nibbles as they flew from the plates. When every last nibble had gone Gustav suggested they moved to the soup course. He was shaking slightly.

"Soup?" Donald turned to Ellie. "I've only ever heard of tomato soup."

"Then, that's what we'll make," Ellie said. "Just tell me what to do."

"How hard can it be?" Donald pondered.
"Tomato soup is just watery tomatoes! You
chop the tomatoes and I'll fill the bowls
with water." Puzzled, Ellie shook her head,
but Gustav had told her to do whatever the
famous chef said.

So the guests were given bowls of water

with chopped tomatoes.

"And now for the magic!" Donald declared.

He planned to delight everyone with his

tablecloth trick. Donald tried to pull the

tablecloths away quickly so everything on

top of the table would stay in place.

But there were clips holding the tablecloths down. When Donald tugged the cloths, everything went everywhere! The salt and pepper flew into the air, along with the olive oil and the flowers. Down they came, sprinkling and spilling into the tomato soup.

CHAPTER FOUR
An Angry Chef

"Perhaps stick to something basic for the next course?" Gustav said with a clenched jaw. He decided he was going to check Martin Banquet's details, to be sure he had the right chef.

"How about pasta?" Donald said to Ellie.

"Pasta isn't very posh," Ellie shrugged.

"You'll have to make it original."

Donald agreed that he should create some
interesting flavours to go with the pasta,
so he made a sauce using every ingredient
he could find.

"Are you sure you want the mustard?"

Ellie asked. "And the peas?"

"Yes, yes. Put them all in. This next

course is going to be colourful."

As the waiters lined up to take the plates, Donald approached the restaurant guests with a pretend-serious face. The kids always used to find that funny.

"Now, it is very important that you eat the pasta like this,"

he said.

Donald picked up a pasta tube and blew through it, making a funny

noise. It sounded a bit like a kazoo.

"The more noise, the better," he said sternly.

He crept back to the kitchen, chuckling, but the guests were alarmed. A few were even a bit scared. They had started to think he was a little mad. They didn't want him to get cross, so they agreed to do exactly what he told them to do.

Everyone blew through their pasta tubes, making the silliest noises possible. Some screamed as their best clothing got splattered with the colourful sauce. Others started laughing. Some couldn't stop laughing! Some played tunes on their pasta kazoos. There was a chaos of noise and colour.

Gustav remained quiet, but his face grew
red as tomato ketchup. He had now
discovered his mistake – there was not a
famous chef in his kitchen, but a children's
entertainer. And not a very good one! He
ordered the waiters to clear the tables and
bring coffees. He would skip the dessert
course. He couldn't risk another disaster.

But Donald was already making pancake batter in the kitchen. He made excellent pancakes, and he had just thought of an entertaining way to serve them.

"Come on, Ellie," Donald said. "We'll toss the pancakes at the table. Let's give them a show!" Ellie, who was now enjoying herself, wheeled out a portable cooker with a pancake pan and batter.

"No, no, NO!" Gustav said, about to explode. "This must stop!"

"But Tartan Blanket's pancakes are the best in the world!" said Donald, and before Gustav could say another word Donald began flipping his pancakes.

Although he was very good at pancake batter, he wasn't very good at pancake tossing. The pancakes flew high into the air and stuck to the ceiling, directly above the guests' heads. One by one, the pancakes fell back down. They fell straight into the coffee cups. Some fell straight onto the faces of the guests. In all the commotion, nobody noticed a new guest at the door.

"Enough!" screeched Gustav. The room fell silent. He pointed to the large man in the doorway. "This is Martin Banquet, famous chef. You, sir, are an imposter!" He pointed a long skinny finger at Donald.

"But I was invited!" Donald protested.

"How dare you pretend to be me! I'll make sure you never cook – or entertain – in this town again!" boomed Martin Banquet.

"Not so fast," came a voice from the back of the room.

CHAPTER FIVE
Back to the Party

Antonio Maccaronio slowly got to his feet.

"When I opened The White Apron it was a family restaurant, where people could eat, relax and laugh. For fifty years I have watched this restaurant get snootier and snootier, and I hate it!"

"We just wanted this to be a s-s-special celebration," Gustav stuttered.

"The nibbles reminded me of apple-bobbling when I was young," sighed an old lady.

"The tomato salad with flower garnish was lovely," said a woman, dabbing her lips with a napkin.

Gustav gasped. "But what about the mess?"

"Well, I won't be cleaning my suit," said a famous doctor. "The colours are exquisite. It will be a memento of a wonderful evening!"

"The pancakes in coffee was genius," added Antonio Maccaronio. "My dear wife got one in the face, but what fun! In my house it will be known as an In-Your-Face-Pancake from now on. Tartan Blanket, what you have done here is marvellous."

The room erupted in applause and Gustav bowed, as if he had arranged it all. Ellie gave him a little kick in his bottom.

"Why don't you say something nice to Mr Tartan Blanket?" she whispered.

Gustav coughed and stepped forward.

"From now on, we'd like to invite Mr Tartan Blanket to host a nibbles night once a month at The White Apron."

The guests whistled and clapped. Martin Banquet stormed out.

"Thank you," Donald nodded. "But I'm a calamitous cook. I think it would be safer for everyone if I went back to children's parties."

Donald got into a taxi with his costume and his bag of juggling balls and spinning plates, and gave the driver an address.

The taxi pulled up outside an enormous mansion.

"Here it is, sir – Maccaronio Mansion."

"The Maccaronio mansion?" Donald gulped.

So the birthday girl was Flavia, the great granddaughter of Antonio Maccaronio! Donald put on his tartan hat and tartan blanket and knocked on the big door and hoped there wouldn't be eggs.

Maccaronio
Mansion

As usual he was a terrible entertainer.

He told bad jokes, spun wobbly plates and

twisted balloons into shapes no one

recognised. And as usual, there was a food

fight to finish it off.

"Oh, Tartan Blanket …" taunted Flavia,

approaching him with an egg in each hand.

"No! Please don't!" Donald pleaded.

"Come on girls!" Flavia called behind her.

Other girls stepped forward with wicked

grins. They were armed with a bag of flour,

a pint of milk, some vanilla ...

"Let's get him," Flavia called, "to make us

an In-Your-Face-Pancake!"

Text © Rachel Delahaye 2016
Illustrations © Janet Cheeseman 2016

The rights of Rachel Delahaye to be
identified as the author and Janet
Cheeseman as the illustrator of this Work
have been asserted in accordance with the
Copyright, Designs and Patents Act, 1988.

Series Editor: Melanie Palmer
Series Advisor: Catherine Glavina
Cover Designer: Cathryn Gilbert
Design Manager: Peter Scoulding

A CIP catalogue record for this book is
available from the British Library.

ISBN 978 1 4451 4994 3 (hbk)
ISBN 978 1 4451 4996 7 (pbk)
ISBN 978 1 4451 4995 0 (library ebook)

Printed in China

Franklin Watts
An imprint of Hachette Children's Group
Part of The Watts Publishing Group
Carmelite House
50 Victoria Embankment
London EC4Y 0DZ

An Hachette UK Company
www.hachette.co.uk

www.franklinwatts.co.uk

MIX
Paper from
responsible sources
FSC® C104740